. pace—in terms of speech, critical thinking, and, of c_. _ng. Penguin Young Readers recognizes this fact. As a result, each Penguin Young Readers book is assigned a traditional easy-to-read level (1–4) as well as a Guided Reading Level (A–P). Both of these systems will help you choose the right book for your child. Please refer to the back of each book for specific leveling information. Penguin Young Readers features esteemed authors and illustrators, stories about favorite characters, fascinating nonfiction, and more!

The Loopy Coop Hens

LEVEL **2**

GUIDED
READING **G**
LEVEL

This book is perfect for a **Progressing Reader** who:
- can figure out unknown words by using picture and context clues;
- can recognize beginning, middle, and ending sounds;
- can make and confirm predictions about what will happen in the text; and
- can distinguish between fiction and nonfiction.

Here are some **activities** you can do during and after reading this book:
- Character Traits: Come up with a list of words to describe Midge, Dot, and Pip. Then come up with a list of words to describe Rooster Sam.
- Compare/Contrast: Compare the list you made for Midge, Pip, and Dot to the list you made for Rooster Sam. How are they alike? How are they different?
- Make Connections: The hens wish they could fly, but flying is hard to do. Still, they never stop trying. Have you ever practiced something that was hard for you to do—and gotten better at it?

Remember, sharing the love of reading with a child is the best gift you can give!

—Bonnie Bader, EdM
   Penguin Young Readers program

*Penguin Young Readers are leveled by independent reviewers applying the standards developed by Irene Fountas and Gay Su Pinnell in *Matching Books to Readers: Using Leveled Books in Guided Reading*, Heinemann, 1999.

For my mom —JMS

Penguin Young Readers
Published by the Penguin Group
Penguin Group (USA) Inc., 375 Hudson Street, New York, New York 10014, USA
Penguin Group (Canada), 90 Eglinton Avenue East, Suite 700, Toronto, Ontario M4P 2Y3, Canada
(a division of Pearson Penguin Canada Inc.)
Penguin Books Ltd., 80 Strand, London WC2R 0RL, England
Penguin Group Ireland, 25 St. Stephen's Green, Dublin 2, Ireland (a division of Penguin Books Ltd.)
Penguin Group (Australia), 250 Camberwell Road, Camberwell, Victoria 3124, Australia
(a division of Pearson Australia Group Pty. Ltd.)
Penguin Books India Pvt. Ltd., 11 Community Centre, Panchsheel Park, New Delhi—110 017, India
Penguin Group (NZ), 67 Apollo Drive, Rosedale, Auckland 0632, New Zealand
(a division of Pearson New Zealand Ltd.)
Penguin Books (South Africa) (Pty.) Ltd., 24 Sturdee Avenue,
Rosebank, Johannesburg 2196, South Africa

Penguin Books Ltd., Registered Offices: 80 Strand, London WC2R 0RL, England

The Library of Congress has catalogued the Dutton edition
under the following Control Number: 2010013354

ISBN 978-0-448-46272-1

10 9 8 7 6 5 4 3 2 1

The Loopy Coop Hens

by Janet Morgan Stoeke

Penguin Young Readers
An Imprint of Penguin Group (USA) Inc.

The Hens

Midge and Pip and Dot are hens.

They live on Loopy Coop Farm.

They love Rooster Sam.

Rooster Sam is tall.

His tail is snowy white.

And his toes are

golden yellow.

But best of all, Rooster Sam can fly!

The hens cannot fly.

They have tried.

But flying is hard to do.

They ask Rooster Sam
how he does it.

But Rooster Sam does not

give them any tips.

His golden toes kick up the sand.

His snow-white tail goes

this way and that.

And he struts away.

The Moth

"Look," says Midge.

"Even this moth can fly."

"That moth is so little!" says Pip.

"It's not fair."

"We're big," says Dot.

"We should be able to fly."

"We have big toes

for pushing off!" says Pip.

"We have big wings, too!"

says Midge.

"Let's do it!"

Oh. Oh. Oh.

Ow. Ow. Ow.

"Well, we still have wings,"

says Midge.

"And we still have toes," says Pip.

"Hmmm.

And beaks!" says Dot.

Rooster Sam

Every morning, Rooster Sam

goes up on the roof.

That is his spot.

He likes to say "Wake UP!"

"Cock-a-doodle-doo!"

The hens wake up when he crows.

They like to see him

high up on the roof.

They see his snow-white tail.

They see his red comb.

They see his neck stretch

w-a-a-a-y out when he crows.

He is their Rooster Sam.

And . . .

he can fly.

But the hens have never
seen him fly.

"He must fly," says Midge.

"He is way up there."

"Let's watch him fly," says Pip.

"We can copy him."

"Then WE can fly!"

The Plan

So they get up early.

They hide.

They watch Rooster Sam.

Rooster Sam does not see them.

They see Rooster Sam

walk to the back of the barn.

They watch him.

He hops onto the truck.

He hops onto the hay.

And then he hops

onto the roof.

Then he stands up tall on the

roof and crows.

Rooster Sam does not fly at all!

Friends

"He didn't fly," says Midge.

"He hopped," says Pip.

"And then he walked," says Dot.

"But you know," says Midge.

"His toes are golden yellow."

"And his comb falls just so,

over one eye," says Pip.

"And his tail is as white

as snow," says Dot.

"Yes," they say.

They love their

Rooster Sam.

[8]